Joshua's Amazing Adventures

Go where your song guides you ™

By Dietrich Thompson

Illustrated by Amitabha Naskar

&

Cover design by: Randy Knoble

A sample of the songs integrated into the story can be heard on http://dietrichthompson.com/

The first book Joshua's Amazing Gift is also available. Learn more at the Author website. http://dietrichthompson.com/

Special Thanks to:

Elisabeth Thompson, Mary Riordan, & Jea McLean

This book is dedicated to Dr. Daniel Riordan. "Thank you for all your guidance and encouragement."

Song: In My Little Dream

By: Dietrich Thompson
Verse I:
In my little dream,
I get inspired by many things.
In my little dreams,
I'm bigger than what I seem.
I'm gonna follow my dreams
Amazing melodies I sing, so
let me dream on, let me be strong, ooh dream, dream.
Verse II:
In my little dream,
I see wonderful possibilities.
In my little dream,
I see all that I could be.
Love the beauty in my dreams;
A new hue in my view. So,
let me dream on, let me be strong, ooh dream, dream.
Bridge:
Daddy said a dream is where it starts.
Momma said follow your heart.
So I dream on, and on, on and on,
pour it all in a song.
(Instrument Verse III)
I'm gonna follow my dreams
Amazing melodies I sing, so
let me dream on, let me be strong, ooh dream, dream.
Verse IV:
In my little dream,
I mirror the wonders that God made
In my little dreams,
Mom and Dad's smile never fade.
So I live life out loud.
They look at me, so proud. So,
let me dream on,
let me be strong, ooh dream
Bridge:
Outro:

Song: Dad and I

By Dietrich Thompson

Verse 1:
Dad and I
built this ship.
Gonna make it fly,
I can't wait to take this trip.

Watch us fly, ooh so high.
Watch us zoom, zoom, zoom in our Rocket Ship.

Verse 2:
Dad and I,
built this ship.
Gonna make it fly,
I can't wait to take this trip.

Watch us fly, ooh so high.
Watch us zoom zoom zoom, and dip, dip, dip. dip dip.

Bridge:
Oh, let me show you, which planet I wanna go to.
Maybe, Venus or Mars, we'll see brand new stars.
Oh, let me show you, which planet I wanna go to.
Let's fly higher, so much higher.

Song: In the Jungle

By Dietrich Thompson

Verse 1:

(2X)
In the jungle, we hear the lions go
They say, roar, roar, roar.

Big elephants, can't be ignored
Hear them stomp their big feet to the floor.

In the Jungle, we see the monkey's swing,
from tree too, tree.

A jungle adventure is happening.
There's so much to hear and see.

Verse 2:

In the jungle, I see gorillas
hanging out, with orangutans.
They, like to party.
And dance and swing.

Ooh, I see Gorillas, hanging out, with orangutans.
They, like to party.
And dance and swing.

Bridge:

Come on a go with me.
Come and go with me.
There is so much to see, so come on and go with me.

Song: Sail the Seven Seas

By Dietrich Thompson

Verse 1:

Let's go sail the seven seas, dig the pirates that you see.
As a team we are at our best, we can find that treasure chest.

Let's go sail the seven seas, friendly pirates is who we be.
Work hard, no time for rest, we gonna find that treasure chest.

Bridge 1:

Ahoy Mateys, Ahoy
Ahoy Mateys, Ahoy

Verse 2:

Let's go sail the seven seas, dig the pirates that you see.
As a team we are at our best, we can find a treasure chest.

Let's go sail the seven seas, dig the pirates that you see.
As a team we are at our best, we can find a treasure chest.
(X2: Shiver, shiver, shiver, shiver me timbers)
(Yeah, Yeah)

Bridge 2:

Blow, Blow, Blow me down
Search for the gold underground.
Blow, Blow, Blow me down
Join the team and help us out.

Joshua's Amazing Adventures

One early Saturday morning Joshua opened his eyes and heard his mother humming a morning medley. She liked to do that in the morning. "Time to get up, Joshua. "She called. But he was dreaming. Joshua softly sang, "In my little dreams, I'm inspired by many things. In my little dreams I'm bigger than what I seem."

Mom leaned into his room, smiled and joined in. "I'm gonna follow my dreams. Amazing melodies I sing, so let me dream on, let me be strong, ooh dream, dream."

After Mom left, Grandma came in and asked, "Joshua, are you ready to get up?"

Joshua turned in his warm and toasty bed and said, "These are my favorite PJs, and I don't want to get up, Grandma."

Suddenly, a big smile popped into Joshua's room and asked excitedly, "Do you want to help me finish building the table buddy?" Joshua liked helping his father build stuff. So, he said, "Sure Dad, but I want to dream a little longer."

Joshua dreamed of an adventure-- he and his Dad building a rocket ship to fly to another planet. Soon Joshua started sing his dream. "Dad and I, built this ship, going to make it fly. I can't wait to take this trip. Watch us fly, oh so high. Watch us zoom, zoom, zoom in our rocket ship."

Then Joshua remembered, " Astronauts wear space suits and boots, not pajamas and fluffy doggy slippers."

Joshua turned over again in his bed and saw toy animals from Africa. He dreamed he and his friends Alejandro, Kevin, and Mary were on an adventure to protect the amazing jungle animals of Africa.

Excited, Mary began to teach them the jungle adventure song. "In the jungle, We hear Lions roar! Roar! Roar! Roar! Big Elephants, can't be ignored, stomping big feet on the floor. In the jungle, see Monkeys swing from tree to tree. A jungle adventure is happening for you and me."

Wait! Jungle Adventurers wear jungle boots, not toasty doggy slippers.

Grandma peaked into Joshua's room a second time with a broad grin, and asked. "Are you ready?"

Joshua said, "I'm still dreaming"

Joshua's sister Zoë, leaned into the bedroom and asked, "Joshua come get your Pirate ship out of the bathtub, please."

What if Joshua, Grandma, his friends and his sister Zoë were sailing the seven seas? He thought, "I would be the captain of the mighty ship."

"Ahoy!" said Zoë, "let's go find a treasure." Then she sang," Let's go sail the seven seas. Dig the Pirates that we be. As a team we're at our best, we can find a treasure chest."

Wait! He didn't know if the captain of pirate ship could bring Thurston, his stuffed puppy. What if Thurston got wet?

Then Joshua thought that if he wanted to have a true adventure, he'd have to leave his favorite pajamas, his toasty doggy slippers and Thurston in his bedroom.

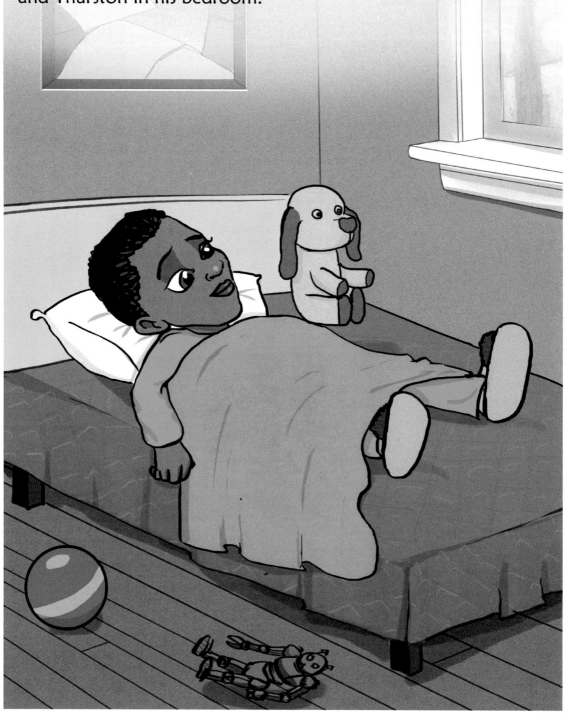

Grandma returned and asked a third time, "Are you ready?"

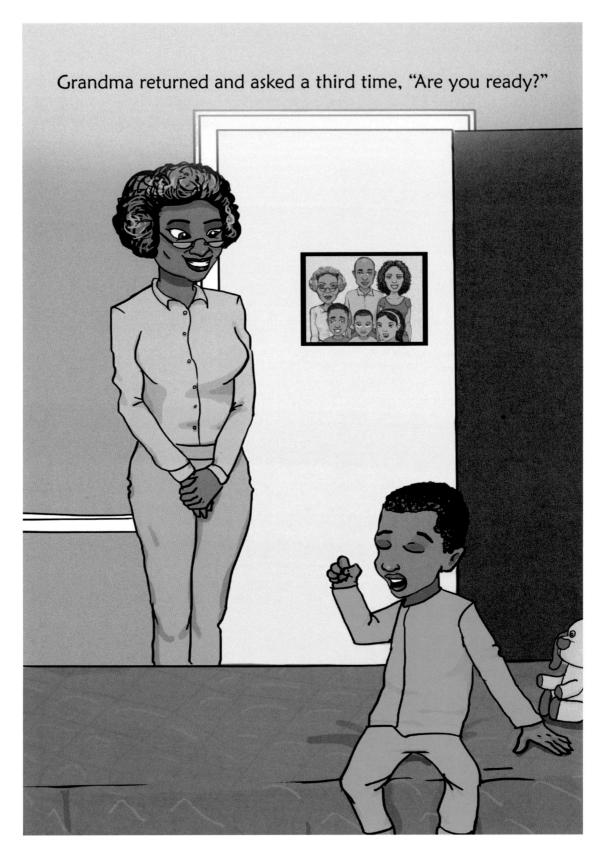

Excitedly, Joshua said, "Yes, I'm ready for an Amazing Adventure!" and he climbed out of bed.

❖ Published by Artifex Soul Publishing
914 164th ST SE
Ste B12 #231

Mill Creek, WA 98012

❖ Author: Dietrich Thompson
❖ Book Illustrations by Amitabha Naskar
❖ Book Cover & original character illustrator, Randy Knoble

❖ Edited by Dr Dan Riordan, and Mary Riordan.

❖ Summary: A young boy must decide if he is going to continue to dream amazing adventures or get up and live an amazing adventure.

❖ The illustrations were executed in Adobe Photoshop
❖ The font was set to Maiandra GD

❖ {1.Family-fiction. 2. Problem solving- Fiction. 3.Multiculral- Fiction.}

❖ ISBN-13: 978-0997739510
❖ ISBN-10: 0997739517
❖ LCCN: 2017917333
❖ Copywrite pending

❖ TM Pending

Made in the USA
Middletown, DE
18 September 2019